A hare lived in a forest by the sea.
She loved her quiet home.
She loved the creek
and the deer who came to drink there.
She loved to sit on a rock,
munching a reed and listening
to bird songs.
The hare was very happy,
until one day . . .

. . . a grumpy giant with blue hair
came to live on a nearby peak.
Every day he would tromp
through the forest
and down to the sea
to catch fish.
Then he would tromp back again.

Every morning the hare would peek
out of her hole
and see the giant's blue hair
above the trees.
She would hear his huge boots
tromping across the creek.
As he walked,
the boots would go *creak, creak,*
scaring the mice and deer and birds.
"Oh, dear!" said the hare.
"This has got to stop!"

She took a reed,

dipped it in some mud,

and made a sign for the giant to read:

NO CREAKY BOOTS, PLEASE!

She carried the sign to the foot of the peak

and stuck it by the path.

Then she hid where she could peek out.

Along came the giant
with his boots going *creak, creak*.
He looked at the sign
and scratched his hair.
"Oh, dear!" said the hare.
"He can't read!
And he is so big and scary,
I am afraid to talk to him.
What will I do?"

She followed the giant
up the peak to his cave.
When he began to snore,
she crept inside to peek around.
The giant was taking a nap.
His feet stuck out of the bed.
They were sore from his boots.
"Oh, dear!" said the hare.
"That poor giant!"
Suddenly she had an idea.

She ran outside and called her friends.
They all came to the cave.
The mice brought fur from their nests.
The birds brought feathers from their wings.
The deer brought hair from their tails.
The little hare stuffed everything
into the giant's boots to make soft pads.
When the animals were done,
they hid.

The giant opened his eyes.
He got out of bed
and put his feet in his boots.
Suddenly he smiled.
He took a step. His smile got bigger.
The boots didn't creak anymore!
The animals cheered.
Now the giant could walk to the sea.
His creaky boots would not scare them.
His feet would not hurt.
And he would no longer be grumpy.